This edition produced for The Book People Ltd, Hall Wood Avenue,
Haydock, St Helens, WA11 9UL

First published in Great Britain by HarperCollins Publishers Ltd in 2000

1 3 5 7 9 10 8 6 4 2
ISBN: 0 00 762731 9

Picture Lions is an imprint of the Children's Division, part of HarperCollins Publishers Ltd

Text and illustrations copyright © Nick Butterworth 2000
The author asserts the moral right to be identified as the author of the work

The HarperCollins website address is: www.fireandwater.com

Manufactured in China

OWL TAKES CHARGE

NICK BUTTERWORTH

TED SMART

"Ooof, you're heavy," gasped Percy the park keeper. Carefully, he lifted a small tree into his wheelbarrow. "Still, you'll look very nice near my . . . aah, ahh, A-TISHOO!"

"Oh dear," said Percy. "I hope I'm not getting a cold."

ercy began to rake over the bare earth where the little tree had been. Suddenly with a SNAP! his rake broke.

"Oh thump," said Percy. "I'll have to fix you now."

As Percy passed by the playground, he stopped to blow his nose.

"Dear, dear," he sighed. "Look at that. The roundabout needs painting. There's so much to do."

"Hello, Percy," said the owl, suddenly landing next to him. "How are you today?"

Percy sneezed again.

"I think I must have a cold coming," he said.

"Then you should be in bed," said the owl. "Come along."

"Don't fuss," said Percy, "I feel . . ."

"No arguments," said the owl firmly. "Into bed with you, now."

"But there's so much to do," groaned Percy. "I've got to make a new rake. I've got to plant that tree, and I've got to paint the roundabout..."

"Now don't you worry, Percy," said the owl. "I'll take care of everything."

Percy closed his eyes.

O utside Percy's hut
the owl stopped
for a moment.

"Now what did he say? Make. Paint. And plant. Yes, I think that was it."

She looked around and saw the little tree and Percy's rake.

"Ah, yes. Tree. Rake. Roundabout."

The owl was very kind but she was not good at remembering things.

"Um, make a tree. No, that's not it. Paint . . . or was it plant . . . hmm. I think I might need some help."

A little later, Percy woke up and looked out of the window.

Whatever were the mice doing with that paint pot? And where were the rabbits going with his little tree?

Just then, the owl came to visit.

"What's going on?" said Percy.

"Nothing for you to worry about, Percy," said the owl. "Would you like me to fan you with my wings? You look hot."

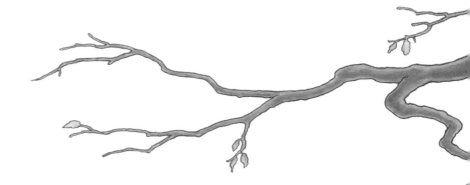

Not far from Percy's hut, the fox and
the badger were hard at work.

"That should hold it," said the badger
as he finished tying a rope around a big
piece of wood.

"Let me try," said the fox.

"Not like that!" laughed the badger.
"Here, I'll show you . . ."

Next morning, Percy was already up and dressed when the owl arrived.

"You look much better," she said.

"I'm fine," said Percy. "I'm never ill for long. There's too much to do. Now where shall I start?"

"Come with me, Percy!" said the owl, proudly. "We've been helping."

"Hello, Percy!" said the rabbits. "We planted your rake. Just like you wanted."

P ercy stood and stared.
   "Er, well, it's very kind of you, but I said *make* a rake not plant it."
   "Oh no, Percy," said the owl. "It wasn't a rake you wanted us to make."
   "What did you make then?"
   said Percy.
   "Come and see,"
   said the owl.

"I don't believe it!" said Percy. "You've made a roundabout!"

"It took us all night," said the fox.

"It's wonderful," said Percy. "But I said *paint* the roundabout, not make one."

"Oh, no," said the owl. "You didn't say paint a roundabout. You said . . ."

Percy looked worried.

"Don't tell me," he said. "You *planted* the rake. You *made* a roundabout. I suppose you must have *painted* my poor little tree!"

"Just like you said!" replied the owl.

At that moment, three giggling mice appeared, carrying a beautiful painting of Percy's little tree.

"Oh, I see!" chuckled Percy. "That's how you painted it! It's lovely. What kind friends you all are."

"Can we go on the roundabout now?" said one of the mice.

"Of course," said Percy.

"Let's give it a spin!"

NICK BUTTERWORTH was born in North London
in 1946 and grew up in a sweet shop in Essex. He now lives
in Suffolk with his wife Annette. They have two grown-up
children, Ben and Amanda.

The inspiration for the Percy the Park Keeper books
came from Nick Butterworth's many walks through the
local park with the family dog, Jake. The stories have sold
nearly three million copies and are loved by children all
around the world. Their popularity has led to the making
of a stunning animated television series, now available on
video from HIT Entertainment plc.

Read all the stories about Percy and his animal friends. . .

then enjoy the Percy activity books.

And don't forget you can now see Percy on video too!